Also available from K. R. Max:

Alphas & Innocents (in ebook only)

Billionaire Santa And His Innocent Intern
Her Dominant Professor
Her Dominant Neighbor
Her Dominant Biker
Her Dominant Lawman

Her Dominant Boss
(in ebook and paperback)

Caden (Her Dominant Boss #1)
Max (Her Dominant Boss #2)

MAX:
Her Dominant Boss #2

K. R. Max

DEDICATION

For my mother, for believing in me and
supporting me when I needed it most

ACKNOWLEDGMENTS

To Leona Bushman-Cunningham,
Dragon Queen of the North.

Max: Her Dominant Boss #2

Shay

I clutch my glass of lukewarm champagne as Harry Hennessy takes the stage. Around me, the employees of Hennessy's Hotel and Conference Center fall silent. We may pretend to be here for the champagne and free buffet, but that's not the real reason.

Well, it's not mine.

Hennessy throws two big parties a year, one in the summer and one at Christmas. It's the beginning of June, schools are out, and we're all gathered on the rooftop terrace at the Carnegie Ridge Park Hotel, ostensibly enjoying the free food and drink.

I've barely eaten anything and the half glass of champagne I knocked back about twenty minutes ago for Dutch courage is already warming my blood. This is it, the moment I've been waiting for, the moment I got a little drunk trying to prepare for. I'm about to finally, *finally*, get the job I really want, the job I've been working towards since graduating high school.

Hennessy looks around and smiles, keen to make us wait, to draw out the tension until someone starts crying. Okay, that would be me. Because I've applied for the Events Coordinator job three times now. They say the third time's the charm, right? I've worked for Hennessy since graduating high school. I know the venue like the insides of my own eyelids. Six years I've worked here, and when the Events Coordinator job first opened up, four years ago, I went for it, only to discover that two years of experience on the job didn't qualify me. So two years ago, when it opened up again, I applied again.

Still not enough experience.

It's been six years. I've been here longer than every other applicant, most of whom applied straight out of college. I've put in immensely long hours and never asked for a raise. I've taken on every challenge that's ever been thrown at me, well, at my manager who then usually passed it down to me, and I triumphed every time. I've got the experience, the client relation skills, and relationships with every vendor in the city who provides products and services for Hennessy events. This job is mine.

Mine.

"I know you're all keen to know who our new Events Coordinator will be, since Mitchell Haynes is now moving on to bigger and better things. So, without further ado, it gives me great pleasure to announce, the new Events Coordinator is…"

Hennessy's eyes land on me and skate away before I can smile in response. Something settles in my belly, cold and hard, and I push the sensation away. This is it. My dream job. Right in the palm of my han—

"Kelley Riker."

I stare at him, then at Kelley's perfect chestnut curls as she bounces up to the stage to shake Hennessy's hand. She turns and smiles at us all, and I want to vomit. She's the same age as me and has been working here for about six months, having bounced around a bit after, as she put it, 'drinking and napping' her way through college. She can't remember anything but never writes anything down. I've ended up doing most of her work as well as mine.

What the *fuck*?

Hennessy steps down off the stage, and I shoulder my way through the crowd to plant myself squarely in front of him. I'm a larger girl, so I'm hard to ignore, but he does his best. Right up to

5

the moment where I lose my patience and grab his arm.

"Mr. Hennessy," I manage to grind out between my teeth, then dial back my temper. I can't yell at my boss. As frustrated as I am in my job, constantly picking up for people who know way less than I do, I do need a job. And I'm good at this one. I just wish someone would actually reward me for that. "Mr. Hennessy, what makes Kelley more qualified than me for the Events Coordinator position?"

He has the grace to look embarrassed, as well he might, since he all but told me the job was mine when I interviewed for it. "I'm really sorry, Shay. I know how much this job would have meant to you, but the fact is, she has a college degree."

I stare at him, my jaw on the floor. "Six years of experience doesn't count for anything?"

"Of course it does, Shay, don't be ridiculous. But I discussed it with the board, and we agreed that college prepares workers for management in a way that experience in lower level positions simply doesn't. I'm very sorry, but that's the policy now."

Spoken like a man who went to college. I blink back the tears, only too aware of what he's saying, what this means for me. I'll never rise above Events Assistant, no matter how much experience I get. And it doesn't matter that six years ago, I was all set to go to Yale.

All that matters to the board is that I didn't go. I didn't graduate. I didn't get a piece of paper which is apparently worth more than all my experience put together. Fury coils in my belly as I realize, once again, my future has been stolen by a man in an expensive suit. Only in this case, I work for the asshole in question.

My jaw tightens. I will not cry in front of this man who thinks I'm some kind of lower class citizen just because I didn't go to college. I won't.

I'll wait until I'm alone in the elevator, like any self-respecting woman.

Of course, standing in the elevator, hot tears running down my face, the door pings open just a few floors down. I scrub my face dry, losing my grip on my purse and sending it crashing to the floor just as the most beautiful man I've ever seen steps inside, wearing a very expensive suit.

***

Max

I do my best to ignore the curvy blonde currently pretending she hasn't just been crying her eyes out as she picks up her things. I can't hold up the pretence for long, though, and I stoop and hand her a dark blue pen which looks as if it's made of glass, then stand and move away. She clearly doesn't want any attention, although I would imagine she's used to receiving it. Even in the hideous skirt suit she's wearing, her body is spectacular enough to turn a man's head at forty paces.

I also didn't miss the way her lip curled when she registered my Kiton suit. I should be glad she's not interested in a man with money, but with a surname instantly recognizable around the world, I'm more intrigued than anything. A woman who doesn't find billionaires attractive? Why aren't there more of those in this city?

I shake my head and force myself to focus on the huge problem my mother just dumped in my lap. Which is actually unfair of me, because it's entirely my fault. If I hadn't been so busy trying to avoid the attentions of my last assistant, I might have realized she wasn't doing the work she was being paid to do. Namely, organize the annual Lupin Family Foundation Midsummer Gala.

Now the gala is three weeks away, and all we have is a venue, and that's only because the foundation has been holding its parties at the same place for over twenty years, so the date is permanently booked. However, nothing else is in place. No vendors, no caterers, *nothing*.

My mother is not pleased.

"I'm not saying you're to blame, Maximilian, but she was your assistant, and I had expected you to take more interest in the organization of this year's gala anyway. Instead, you handed the job off to some floozy who was more interested in landing a rich husband than organizing our biggest fundraising event. I don't need to tell you what the consequences will be if this event doesn't go ahead."

Her words ring in my ears even as the hum of the elevator rises around us. I suddenly realize the mechanical whine has risen to an uncomfortable pitch, but there's no time to question it before there's a crunch and the elevator jerks to a halt. In the same moment, the lights blink out, plunging us into darkness.

"What. The. *Fuck*?"

I smile, even as my cock twitches at the sound of her voice, strong and musical. "Relax," I tell her. "It's probably just a power glitch. The lights will come on again in a second."

Several seconds pass, and I swear I can feel her glaring at me.

"You were saying?"

She swallows, loud enough for me to hear it where I'm standing several feet away, and I realize she's scared. Doing her best to control it, which is admirable, particularly as most women of my acquaintance would be screaming blue murder by now, but still scared.

"Here," I say, "walk towards me."

"Why?"

I've rarely heard a more suspicious tone directed my way. Well, not since I stopped playing pranks on my brothers as a child. Mother would be proud. Forcing myself to repress a sigh, I hold out my hand, then remember she can't see it, which is the problem. God, Lupin, get a grip.

"Because if you're scared of the dark, or small spaces, or both, you can hold my hand, and it will help."

There follows a long silence, then I hear her move. Fabric brushes against my fingertips, but my hand closes on nothing. Instead, I hear her pressing buttons, and I smile. Smart girl. She's bypassed the comfort portion of the evening and has moved straight into problem-solving, in spite of her fear. I'm impressed.

I'm also a little surprised at how disappointed I am. I hadn't realized until this moment how much I was looking forward to experiencing the texture of her skin.

And now my brain has gone somewhere entirely inappropriate, and I'm damn glad it's dark in here.

"Hello, can you hear me?" A disembodied voice addresses us.

"Yes! I mean, yes," she says, lowering her tone from its initial shriek. "The elevator just stopped, and the lights have gone out."

"Okay, I'm really sorry about that. There was some issue with the power, but the lights should have come on again by now. We're checking the emergency generator now. How many of you are in there?"

"Two."

"Any medical issues we should know about?"

"Well it wouldn't do you much good if there were, would it?" she mutters quietly, making me chuckle. Raising her voice, she responds, "No, we're fine."

"Okay. Give us a minute to get the lights back on. I'm waiting on an ETA from the fire department."

"Okay."

Her voice trembles, and this time I can't help myself. I move towards her, and my hand finds her arm. She gasps, then reluctantly reaches for me, her hands brushing down my chest until she suddenly snatches them back. "I'm sorry."

"Don't be. I was enjoying that."

She makes a disgusted sound and goes to pull away, but I keep a firm grip of her arm. Okay, it was an asshole thing to say. I was hoping to lighten the situation with humor. Clearly, that was the wrong way to go.

Still, she may be too proud to want to take comfort from a stranger, but that doesn't mean I won't do what's right. I slide my hand down to hers, then interlock our fingers. There's a click, and suddenly the lights come on. The look on her face is a gift, such relief, and it makes something tighten in my gut. I don't want her to be sad or scared, but I'm not going to think too closely about why. She's not mine to take care of.

Not yet, anyway.

The radio crackles and the tinny voice makes her jump. I rub my thumb over her palm to calm her, and she stares at her hand, then at my face. Her eyes are a luminous green, and I find myself falling into them. She seems just as intent on my face as I am on hers, so that we both miss what's being said by the emergency technician.

"I'm sorry." I suddenly realize someone asked a question. "What was that?"

"I said, it's going to be about an hour before the fire department can get here. Are you guys going to be okay?"

"Yes," I say, without thinking, then I look at her face. The click of the radio going dead emphasizes the lost look in her eyes, and her lips tremble. She looks like she's about to burst into tears, and I can only think of one thing to do about it, which is cover her mouth with mine.

I only meant to distract her, but the moment my lips touch hers, all conscious thought evaporates. Soft and warm and pliant. At first she freezes, but then her mouth opens on a moan, and I need no second invitation. I groan, plunging my tongue into the hot, sweet, welcoming cavern of her mouth, sliding my hands into her hair and tilting her head to give me greater access.

I pull back. She stares at me, confusion filling her eyes. As much as I want to drown myself in her, though, there's one thing I have to know first.

"Yes?" I ask.

She frowns. "Yes, what?"

"Do you want this?" I ask her.I'm a thousand per cent sure she's with me right now, but a gentleman never makes assumptions about such things, and my mother raised me to be a gentleman.

I see the moment where she struggles with her conscience. After all, we're strangers, although not for much longer, if I have anything to say about it.

"Fuck it," she says. "Yes."

I grin, then back her against the wall of the elevator, letting her feel just how much I want her. I smile against her lips as she gasps, then revel in the feel of her hands sliding across my shoulders. She clings to me as her tongue duels with mine, slick heat sliding in my mouth, shooting bolts of sensation right down my spine, straight to my cock.

I move closer and pull her hands off my shoulders, pinning them to the wall above her head so that I can stand back and admire her. Her chest heaves as she gasps for air, and I can barely resist the temptation to rip that ugly, high collared shirt off her and bare her magnificent breasts to my gaze. I am aware, however, that we're in an elevator, not a private home, and we still have to get back to my apartment after we leave here.

It's not a question. I'm already drunk on this woman, and I've barely touched her. An hour isn't going to be enough, and I can tell it's the same for her, too. Her face is flushed, her eyes sparkling with passion, and her body writhes before me, desperate for my touch, her hands tugging at my iron grip. I may not be able to get her naked in here, I do have some standards, and this is my mother's building, but there are other things I can do. Pleasurable things. *Highly* pleasurable things.

I slip my fingers into her collar, and her eyes widen as I free a button, then another, moving south slowly, as slowly as I can, opening her shirt, revealing her smooth, creamy curves. My fingers drift over the upper swells of her breasts, and her eyes drift shut, her head falling back. Then I pinch a hardened nipple through the lace of her bra, and she yelps, her eyes flying open. A moment later, a desperate moan fills the air as I wrap my lips around her nipple and suck.

The tip is hard and swollen between my lips, against my tongue, and it makes me want to bite. So I do, and I'm rewarded with her body jerking against me and another moan which has my cock slamming against my zipper. Damn, this woman is so hot, so needy, and I'm only just getting started.

I pull her bra down and feast on her breast, reveling in the sexy, desperate sounds falling from her mouth. Her body twists against me, pushing her flesh against my tongue, my teeth, and I lick and suck and nibble until she's begging for more.

"You want more, Princess?" I ask her, my voice deeper than usual, rough with the effort of holding back. I want to lift her skirt and drive into her, filling her with my cock until we're both sated and sweaty and exhausted, but I can't. Not here.

"Please," she says again. "Please..."

I'm not sure she even knows what she's saying, but the lady wants more, and far be it from me to deny her. I skim a hand down her body, dipping into the curve of her waist and out again over her hip, then down a firm, lush thigh until I reach the hem of her skirt. I lift it and thank God she's not wearing panty hose. Not that that would have stopped me, but I'd feel bad for ruining her clothes.

Maybe.

I run my fingers up the inside of her thigh, glorying in her soft, smooth skin. Then I raise my head, wanting to see her face as my fingers brush over her core, covered only with a thin layer of soaking wet cotton.

Her eyes fly open, and she jerks against me, my hand and body keeping her firmly imprisoned against the wall.

I take a moment to admire the picture she makes, breasts heaving, pulse pounding at her throat, her skin rosy, just waiting for my touch.

"Perfect," I mutter, sliding a finger under the edge of her panties and dragging it through her wet curls to flick over her clit.

She utters a strangled cry, arching against me, and I press into her, grinding my rigid cock against her hip. I'm no saint. I've been with a few women, women who've been around, women who know the score, but I've never even touched a woman this desperate to feel my hands on her. Desperate for my money, absolutely. But desperate for me, just *me*? Never.

Her face is flushed, her eyes closed once more, her hips moving in rhythm to my hand as I slide my finger back and forth against her heated flesh. I need to see those eyes again, need to see her react as I enter her, as I bring her pleasure.

"Open your eyes for me, Princess," I tell her, gripping her wrists a little tighter when she doesn't initially respond. "Open wide. I want to see those beautiful green eyes."

She opens her eyes, and I slide a finger deep inside her. She wails, and it's all I can do not to come in my pants. She's so tight, so hot, and so responsive as I curl my finger inside her and make her cry out again, writhing against me as I slide in and out, adding another finger, pushing higher and deeper with every stroke. She's begging again, desperate pleas with every breath, gasping and moaning, and I cover her mouth with mine, just to feel her ragged breath in my mouth. My lips move to her throat, licking and nipping at her skin, savoring the taste of her musk and sweat.

Finally, I lift my head and press down on her clit with my thumb, and she spasms around me, her screams of pleasure ringing in the small metal room. Her walls grip my fingers like a vice, clenching hard around me again and again, until finally she falls limp in my grip, quivering, trembling, utterly wrung out.

I stare down at her, and all I can think is, *I can't wait to do that again*.

I slide my fingers out of her and raise them to my nose. Her scent is intoxicating, and I brush the moisture across her lips. "Taste yourself, Princess," I tell her. "Taste yourself on my skin."

She opens her eyes, bright as a cat's, and licks my fingers clean. I swallow hard, the sight of her pink tongue swiping over my flesh doing nothing to help my raging hard on.

A grating noise from above alerts us just before the elevator starts moving again, and I do up her buttons seconds before we reach the first floor. The doors open, and I gesture to her to go ahead of me.

Instead of walking forward, as I expect, she leaps out of the elevator like a gazelle on the

Serengeti, disappearing into the crowd of firefighters and hotel staff in a second. I push through, brushing off the horrified staff, who clearly hadn't realized exactly who was trapped in the elevator, but by the time I'm clear of the crowd, she's gone.

And I didn't even get her name.

***

Shay

I race down the sidewalk, dodging passers-by and looking over my shoulder like I'm running from the cops. Frankly, I'm actually surprised I can run like this. My legs are still trembling from the beautiful stranger's talented touch in the elevator, my core still tingling, my skin overheated and somehow too tight for my body. My pussy aches, like it needs more, although I can't imagine what because I'm pretty sure that orgasm turned me inside out.

It's not that I've never had an orgasm before. I know my way around my body, but I've never got close enough to a guy to get that far. In school, I was studying hard, and I wasn't the type of girl the guys were attracted to anyway.

After that, well, I was working, and there wasn't time for that kind of thing. Even if anyone had looked twice at me which, let's face it, they didn't. In fact, I can't remember the last time anyone even asked me out, let alone looked at me like Tall, Dark and Handsome did; like he was dying of thirst and I was the last Big Gulp on Earth.

When he walked into that elevator, I wanted to hate him, just on principle. His suit had to be worth four times my monthly salary, and we're not even going to talk about his watch. But the way he spoke to me, like I was someone, someone important. I know he saw my nerves. I've never been a huge fan of the dark, and instead of mocking me, he tried to make me feel better.

I slow to a walk because it's even harder to run when you're laughing. He made me feel better, alright. So damn good I screamed. Still, I know running was the right thing to do. He's a rich guy with a charming smile and money to burn. I'm...not. Not rich. Not hot. Even if he'd wanted to make something more of it, how far would we have got?

I know what I am and what I'm not, and under 'Not' is Attractive To Suitable Men. If I'd stayed, even if he wanted more than another notch on his bedpost (or elevator wall), he'd have turned out to be an asshole in the end. They all do. The one time one of the rich kids asked me out in high school, I later found out it was because he was curious about what it would be like to 'do a whale'.

Yeah, I didn't show up for our supposed date, and I never regretted it for a minute. So I'm not going to regret walking out on this guy, either. I'm sure he can find a hundred girls, all far more beautiful than me, probably all professional models or heiresses, or both, right there in his little chick-tionary.

Oh come on. Every guy has a chick-tionary.

I, on the other hand, have a life to change. Mine. Now I know where I stand with Hennessy, it's time to move on. I've got six years experience and a wealth of local knowledge. I may not have a degree, but there must be someone out there who doesn't care about that, who'll see experience as valuable in itself.

I duck into a cafe, order an iced latte to cool down my still feverish body, and start surfing the job sites. An hour later, my ebullient mood is deflating fast. Clearly the post-orgasm high is wearing off, not helped by the fact that everyone wants a goddamn degree.

Then I see it. 'Events Coordinator. Temporary contract, experience required, no degree necessary. Immediate start.' Clearly, whoever this is, is desperate, but that's okay, because I am too. I can't stay at Hennessy now, not without making everyone think it's fine to treat me like the wage slave I am and constantly promote less qualified candidates over my head. This may be a temporary position, but it's got the right job title on it, and that's what I need right now. I compose an email, attach my most recent resume, and fire it off.

Then I order another iced latte, because *damn*, I'm still too hot for my clothes, and that thought triggers the memory of what he was doing under my clothes, and I'm *so ready* when that latte finally arrives. I gulp it down, desperate to cool off. My nipples are engorged, rubbing uncomfortably against my bra, and I'm having to restrain myself from wriggling in my seat to try and ease the tension between my thighs.

The last of the latte trickles down my throat just as there's a *ping* from my phone. I nearly drop it as I stare at the subject line. 'Interview today'. They're calling me in. They're actually calling me in! I open the email and scan it.

Correction: They're calling me in *rightnow*. I've got half an hour to get across town and get myself under some semblance of control. I blink, triple check the email, then leap out of my chair, pay for my coffee, and hurtle out the door to hail a cab.

Interviewing me is an older lady with not a hair out of place. Her perfume smells faintly of gardenias, and she looks like she could shut down a bar fight with a single glare from her steel gray eyes, but she's welcoming and calm and doesn't make me feel like I'm inadequate for not having a goddamn degree.

She offers me some iced water, and I accept gratefully.

"Thanks. It's been kind of a crazy afternoon."

She smiles and hands me the glass, then gives me a moment to sip.

"Now," she says. "First things first. Are you single?"

I almost choke on my water, then stare at her. "What's that got to do with the job?"

She tilts her head. "Nothing whatsoever. Or at least, it shouldn't. But sadly, the gentleman you'll be working for has very bad luck with assistants, and I need to make sure I'm hiring the right one. So, do you have a partner or not?"

"No," I snap. "And I don't intend to. I certainly have no interest in hooking up with some snakeskin-suited money man. I just want to do my job and go home."

Her eyebrows twitch, and now I'm regretting the snakeskin-suit comment. Dammit, I really wanted this job.

"Look," I tell her, standing up and lifting my purse over my shoulder. "I have years of experience and no qualifications. I just learned that my current position is never going to go anywhere, and all I wanted was a shot at proving myself. But if your boss is more concerned with whether or not I'm going to spend all day hitting on him, we're probably not a good match anyway. Thanks for your time."

I turn away, and my heels sink silently into the thick, soft carpet, which is why her voice is clear as a bell when she speaks.

"Can you start now?"

I turn around and stare at her. "Well, technically yes, but I'll lose my pay for my notice period, and I'm afraid—"

"And if Max can reimburse you for that?" She sees the look on my face. "Max is your new boss."

"He is? I mean...you're hiring me?"

The corners of her mouth turn up ever so slightly. "That is why you came to this interview, isn't it?"

"Yes! I mean...yes, of course. I just... Oh hell, whatever. Thank you!" I shake her hand, and she immediately starts telling me about the job.

"The Lupin Family Foundation's annual gala is in a bit of a mess," she says, handing me a binder about three inches thick.

Lupin? As in...? Holy shit. I wanted to get into the big leagues but wow. Talk about be careful what you wish for. I shake my head and focus on the issue at hand. Panic won't help me get the job done,

"Let me guess, the last assistant was single?" I smile up at her, hoping to hide my nerves as I open the binder and scan the contents. My professional brain soon takes over, noting vendors, entertainment options, guest lists. And no current invoices. Shit. This woman did nothing at all. "When is it?"

"It wouldn't have been a problem if she hadn't been so determined to hook herself a rich husband via the office. Midsummer's Eve."

It takes me a moment to realize the last two words are in answer to my query about the date, but then I do the math and look up at her, trying to figure out what the hell's going on.

"Th-This Midsummer's Eve? As in, June twenty-first of this year?"

She nods and grimaces.

"That's three weeks away."

"You see our problem, then?"

"You want me to pull off one of the biggest events in the city in less than a month?" My tone rises, but there's little I can do to pull it back. I wanted a job that used my talents, not mission fricken impossible.

The door opens behind me, whispering over the thick carpet.

"Max," she says, apparently relieved by the distraction. "This is your new Events Coordinator. Shay Thorne, meet Max Lupin."

I turn around, and the third nightmare of the day walks towards me, smiling a familiar smile. He doesn't look nearly as shocked as he could, considering the last time we saw each other, his fingers were still wet from my pussy.

I straighten up, pulling my shoulders back even though all I really want to do is curl into the fetal position and cry at the injustice of it all. My big shot at my dream is the Lupin annual ball, a fairytale affair attended by half the East Coast elite, and a chunk of the West Coast glitterati, too. It's impossible to pull off something like that in less than six months, but I'm going to have to do it in less than one, and I'm going to have to do it all while ignoring the stunningly gorgeous man in front of me who had his hand in my panties the first time we met.

I can do this. I *can* do this.

"Shay Thorne," he says, his tongue wrapping around my name in a way that makes me shiver. "What a pleasure."

I'm *so* screwed.

***

Max

I can't believe my luck. She's here, right in front of me, my dream woman. And she's agreed to work with me for the next three weeks in order to make the gala happen. That gives me three weeks to work on her and persuade her that actually she should give us a chance. I'm many things, but insensitive is not one of them, and she's clearly not as pleased to see me as I am to see her.

That said, I saw her pupils dilate when she first recognized me. She wants me. Whether she's willing to admit it or not is another matter.

I open the office door for her. She looks at it like it's going to bite, but finally, her manners get the better of her, and she walks through, giving me the perfect view of her ass. I didn't get to watch her walk away before. I was too unprepared for her exit to enjoy the view. This time, I give myself a moment to appreciate the perfection in front of me, before refocusing on the back of her head and her glossy hair.

"We're heading straight over to the venue," I tell her. "My mother has asked a number of our regular vendors to meet us there so that we can discuss our needs and see if they can accommodate us."

"At three weeks' notice? Unlikely," she says, and I'm pleased to note her tone. She sounds frustrated but not defeated. It means she's not underestimating the mammoth task ahead of us, but she's not backing from it. I like her spirit. God knows I'm going to need it if we're to get this gala off the ground in time for Midsummer's Eve.

We exit the office building, and I direct her to the curb where my town car is waiting. Brett opens the back door for us, and she looks at me, then at the inside of the car.

"It's just a car, Shay." Then I realize the problem. "We can open the windows if you'd prefer more light. It's the quickest way of getting about town, though, and we need to be at the venue in thirty-five minutes."

She frowns at me, then her face clears. "I'm not that scared of the dark. I just didn't think… Never mind. Don't worry about it."

She slides into the car and folds her legs in after her. I want to run my handover her skin, spread her thighs, and take advantage of the car's privacy glass, but there's a job to be done, and she doesn't trust me anyway.

Yet.

But it's nice to know she'd forgotten I'm a billionaire, between the office and the car. How else would I get around town? Nash, my security consultant, would have a fit if I ditched the very expensive armored vehicles he has made up for me, to his own spec, to gad around town in a cab.

I slide into the car after her, and she squeezes herself up against the opposite door. It rankles a little, but I pretend not to notice. We've got time for her to get used to me, and I'd rather she came around to the idea herself rather than me pushing into her space.

Focusing on the job at hand is easier said than done, though, as we walk into the venue with her lush curves leading the way. I tear my eyes away from her ass and focus on opening doors for her. It seems to irritate her, which I take as a good reason to keep doing it. I'm not about to let her forget me or keep me at a distance. Besides, my mother would have my hide if I didn't open doors for a lady. It's not that I don't think she can do it herself. I just don't think she should have to.

A small, dapper man introduces himself as the manager and leads us through the lobby to the ballroom where we'll be holding the gala. "We were most concerned not to have heard from the Foundation," he says, in between pointing out where the tables and stage and so on usually go. "We did attempt to contact your office several times, but never received a reply."

I shake my head. That's the last damn time I hire my own assistant. Shay's already done more than Cherise ever did. She's already opening up the binder and peppering the manager with questions. I zone out, forcing myself to look around the room rather than at her face, so alive and focused on her work. She clearly knows her stuff, talking about caterers, maximum attendee numbers and accommodations for the band.

None of which have been booked, of course.

I sigh, and she looks over at me. "What's your budget?" she asks, and I smile.

"We've got three weeks to pull off an event which usually takes eight months to plan. Just do what you have to do to get it to work. The cost really doesn't matter at this point."

She gives me a strange look, then turns back to her binder. "Of course it doesn't," she mutters not quite under her breath, shaking her head.

Ah, so that's it. The money. I'd forgotten the way she looked at my suit when we first met. She doesn't like rich guys.

Well, on the one hand, she's shit out of luck, because I'm not about to give away my billions, and my company that makes those billions, just to make her happy. On the other hand, such distaste for the rich has to have come from somewhere, although it seems unusual in a profession expressly designed to cater to the rich. Most people with less money make do without someone else's help to plan their parties.

The most likely explanation is an asshole ex-boyfriend, I reason. After all, looking the way she does, there have to be guys in her past. A pain in my hand alerts me to the fact I'm clenching my fists, my fingernails digging into my palms. I want to hunt down whoever hurt her and make them pay, preferably in blood and teeth. But it's more than that. I want to hurt everyone who ever touched her, everyone who wasn't good enough for her, because if they were, she'd be with them and not here, trying to hide her attraction to me.

Several vendors show up over the course of the next hour, including the same caterer we had last year who, thank God, kept the dates free just on the off chance that there'd been a miscommunication. Shay's astonishment shows, and Ravvi just smiles at her.

"We've been catering this event since it started, nearly twenty-five years ago. I knew it would go ahead, and I know just what Mrs. Lupin likes, so it won't be a problem at all. I took the liberty of coming up with some lovely dishes which I think you'll all appreciate."

She hands us both a copy of the menu, and it looks good to me.

"What do you think?" I ask Shay, who looks like she wants to eat the card the menu's printed on.

"It looks amazing," she says, making notes with her blue pen. She looks around, rather wistfully, and I kick myself as I realize, rather belatedly, she must be starving hungry.

"I don't suppose you brought samples," I ask Ravvi, knowing her well enough by now to figure it's a possibility.

She brightens even further. "Of course! Be seated." It's an order, not a request, and we sit as multiple tiny dishes appear on the table. I make sure Shay tries something of everything, insisting she sample things first, 'just in case'.

"Just in case what? The amazing chef who's been catering your family's flagship party for two and a half decades randomly picks today to poison you?" she scoffs.

"Yes," I tell her, and she rolls her eyes. I'm not fooled, though. I see the spark in her eyes, the twitch in her lips. I want to kiss that sassy mouth, to see her eyes widen as I slide inside her…

I take a breath and slide the napkin firmly into my lap in an effort to hide the growing situation down there. Shay doesn't appear to notice, but Ravvi smirks as she gathers up the plates.

"Would you like to keep the napkin?" she asks. "Maybe as a sample for the color scheme?"

I slide her a sideways look, but she just smiles, utterly unrepentant. Damn. My mother's going to hear about this, and then I'm going to get another ear-bashing. I look over at Shay, who looks well-fed, sighing with satisfaction as she hands her plate back to Ravvi.

Whatever my mother heaps on my ears, it'll be worth it. Shay deserves to be looked after, taken care of. She wriggles in her chair, making her breasts bounce under her shirt, before picking up the binder and addressing the latest vendor to arrive.

Beautiful, focused, and organized. She's absolutely worth it.

***

Shay

I don't like this guy.

Not Max, although he's also irritating, albeit in a totally different way. No, the guy who's pissing me off even more right now, which I didn't think was possible, is Shane Critterbuck. He of the ridiculous name, which I can't blame him for, and total asshole attitude, for which I absolutely can. He's been here a good five minutes, and he hasn't made eye contact with me once.

When Max introduced me as the organizer of the event, Shane's eyes swept over me, lingered on my breasts, then slid away. No eye contact, no greeting, and all his responses to my questions have been directed at Max. This asshole is not worth my time. Unfortunately, he's supposed to be the best florist in the city, and the Lupin summer gala always has the most amazing fresh flowers. I figure I'm stuck with this dick whether I like it or not.

"We're aiming for a cream and blue color scheme," I tell him. "Is that something you can accommodate?"

"I'd have to check with our suppliers," he says to Max, and my temper boils over.

"I'm over here," I snarl, finally losing my few remaining shreds of patience. It's been a rough day. I'm tired. I'm stressed. I'm completely overwhelmed. And this piece of shit is treating me like I'm nothing more than pornographic wallpaper.

He finally looks over at me, his eyes immediately falling to my chest. "I prefer to communicate directly with the event organizer, little lady. It avoids miscommunication further down the line."

I stare at him. Did he just imply that I can't do my job? That I'm not intelligent enough to grasp the details? What does he think the fucking binder's for? I could anchor the USS Constitution with this thing.

I open my mouth to put him straight, then reconsider. I don't want to piss off the florist, but more than that, am I sure I can do this job? It's huge, insanely so, and I've never handled an event of this size, not on my own. Max is being very attentive, and honestly, that's confusing me more than the way my body lights up around him. His touch makes me tremble, and his eyes set my pussy alight, but at the end of the day, I am just an employee, right? He hasn't said anything so far. Maybe he agrees with this dickwad.

I lift my chin. I'm not going to make a scene, and he knows it. I see the victory in his eyes, and I want to slap him, but instead I cringe. Maybe I'm not cut out for this job after all, if this is the kind of assholery I'm going to have to deal with.

"She is the organizer," Max says, taking us both by surprise. Doubt flickers in Critterbuck's eyes.

"I—"

"I did tell you that when you arrived," Max continues, his tone almost lazy, but I can hear the cutting edge underneath. "If you can't keep even that basic information straight, maybe you shouldn't be pitching your services for this event. We require absolute up to the minute organization, especially given the special circumstances surrounding this year's gala. We can only work with the best."

Critterbuck's mouth opens and closes a few times. He finally stammers out a few words of apology and proceeds, finally, to talk to my face for the next five minutes while I tell him exactly what we want, how much, and where. And just because he deserves it, when he tells me how much it's going to cost, I tell him he's giving us a fifteen percent discount, for the privilege of us using his services.

It's a bitchy thing to do, but he clearly values Lupin business, and I figure it's the only truly effective way to punish his butthead attitude towards me. Still, I'm actually astonished when he agrees.

He leaves, having signed the service agreement so there's no wriggling out of it later, and I sit there, trying to get my breath back. Did I just do that? More to the point, Max totally had my back. I wasn't expecting that. Turns out he's not just good at providing orgasms. He's been taking care of me in every possible way today, making sure I eat and drink, as well as backing me up with misogynistic suppliers.

I'm not going to look at him right now. I'm not going to respond to his protectiveness. I should have stood up for myself, and he did it for me, and I'm grateful, but I can't afford to let this color how I feel about him.

And how do you feel about him?

The tiny voice inside isn't as easy to squash as I'd like. The more time I spend around Max, the more I see of the man I'd like to know, instead of the suit he's wearing. And it scares me how much I like the man, because the suit comes as part of the deal, and I'm not sure I can handle that.

"That's everyone for today," he says, startling me out of my thoughts. I turn to see him standing up, and when he holds out a hand to help me up, I take it without thinking.

It's a mistake. His warm, strong fingers closing around mine sends heat through my body, unfurling in my veins to warm me through and through. It's not just the tension in my belly, making my hyper-aware of him. It's the sense of safety and security I feel. I shouldn't feel that, not with him. He's my boss, for crying out loud.

And yet...

We enter the elevator, and he presses the button for the first floor, then turns, and suddenly, I'm pressed up against the wall, my wrists pinned above my head, his other hand wrapped around my throat, his breath on my lips, and his cock hard against my belly. He brushes his mouth over my jaw and up my neck, and I quiver against him, my blood turning to quicksilver at his touch.

"Don't ever let anyone talk to you like that again," he mutters in my ear. "You're worth a thousand of any of them."

I gasp for breath, unable to string together a coherent thought, let alone a response, and then he steps back, and the door opens. He gestures for me to precede him out of the lift, and I do so, rather unsteadily. I'm so turned on I can barely walk, and I can feel his eyes boring into my back. I want nothing more than to turn around, push him back inside the elevator, and beg him to take me, but instead, I walk to the town car. Professional. Cool. Calm. Collected.

At least that's how I hope I look on the outside. Inside, I'm anything but, more like a volcano on the verge of erupting. And I can't do that. I can't afford to. Not if I want to pull this job off successfully. My entire career is riding on it, far too much to risk for a fling with my boss.

***

Max

Another day, another disaster. If I were the blackballing kind, I'd make sure Cherise never got hired again in this city. Possibly any city. At least, not in the circles I run in, and that she was looking to marry into.

I end the call on my cellphone and look over at my new assistant, struggling to hold onto my temper. "The gallery which was going to supply pieces for the silent auction never received confirmation, so we have nothing to auction."

Shay looks over at me, clearly confused. She leafs through the binder. "Silent auction? Is that normal?"

I smile. She already knows that thing back to front. She must be studying it at night, and the idea of her sitting in bed with that massive binder in front of her and some hideous nightgown on makes my cock surge. I swallow and shift in my chair, thankful we're sitting at a table in the venue's grand ballroom, so she can't see the erection tenting my pants.

"No. It was Mother's idea. She wanted something a little different this year. She likes to keep it fresh, make it an event people want to come to because it's always changing, always a new approach, rather than the same old cap in hand, year after year."

She smiles, and my breath locks in my throat. She has no idea how beautiful she is when she does that. I see her smile a lot, of course, but mostly it's directed at the suppliers. The old saying about honey and vinegar is absolutely right. She's got people agreeing to things that would normally take six months to arrange. Evidently, she's built up a whole lot of goodwill in this city through her other job. They were fools not to promote her while they had the chance.

This smile, though, this is for me. One hundred per cent, full wattage, beaming out of her whole face, and all for me.

Damn, I want her.

"I like your mother. I mean, I've never met her, but I like her."

It takes me a second to remember what we were talking about, and then it comes back to me. Okay, fine, I admit it. The smile is for my mother, but she's not here, and I am. You snooze, you lose.

"She's a fine woman. Runs the foundation like a military operation."

Her smile is wistful, and I realize there's a story there. A week ago I wouldn't have pushed, but I want to know Shay, the *real* Shay. I want to peel back all the layers and lay her mystery bare. She intrigues me, in a way no woman has in as long as I can remember. I want to know all her secrets.

"What's your mother like?"

Her eyes meet mine for a second before sliding away. For a moment, I think she's going to lie to me, but then her gaze returns. "She passed away a few years ago. She was never...the same after my dad left."

"I'm sorry. I had no idea."

She smiles ruefully. "That my mom was dead, or that my dad abandoned us?"

"Both," I manage. It's a double gut punch, and I deserve it. She's only twenty-four, I know that much from her resume, which I had Caden's office manager send to me the day she hired Shay. This girl's been on her own for a while. No wonder she's nervous of letting people in. She's got no backup for if things go wrong. *When* they go wrong.

I hate knowing things have gone wrong, and I wasn't there to help.

"You mean you didn't do a full background check on me before agreeing to hire me?" she asks, her tone teasing, but I sense something else going on there, a brittle edge to the words. "Shame on you, Max Lupin. So lax with your security. What would Nash say?"

I've told her a bit about Nash. She knows he's handling security for the gala, but she hasn't met him yet.

"That I'm a naive fool who trusts people too easily," I tell her, lightly. The cloud that falls over her face takes me by surprise. Evidently, I've touched a nerve, and I want to push harder, but I don't want to see her sad. I'm ready to change the subject, and I'm surprised when she speaks.

"My dad got conned by a man in a sharp suit and a ready smile," she says, her eyes meeting mine. Candid. Direct. I'd be pleased, except I think I'm about to find out why she hates my money so much, and I have a feeling I'm not going to like it.

"It was a new startup," she continues. "Guaranteed to make it big. All he needed was seed money. Dad reckoned he could double or even triple my college fund. I'd been accepted to Yale, you see, was heading there in the fall. Even got a partial ride, but even so, Yale's expensive. They had enough money for me to go, but it would be tight. This way, I wouldn't have to worry, and neither would they. It was the perfect solution."

Icy snakes slither in my gut. I've heard this story before, too many times. "The company failed?"

She blinks at me, like she'd forgotten I was there, like she wasn't seeing me but someone else, from a long time ago. "Oh no. The company couldn't fail, because it didn't exist. No product, no service. Just my dad and a couple hundred other chumps all looking to make a quick buck."

And suddenly, it all becomes clear. Why she hates rich men. It makes sense now, in a way it didn't before. Whoever took her dad for a ride didn't just take his money. He stole Shay's future. With a degree, she'd have been running events for years by now. Without it, she was dependent on whoever was hiring, and their policies for what constituted management material. I shook my head. It shouldn't have held her back, but some people just had to see the piece of paper.

"I'm sorry. I didn't realize."

She takes a deep breath and stares at the binder for a moment before looking up at me. "It's okay. You're not him."

She shrugs and watches the staff setting up tables at the other end of the room. They're testing out napkin folds today, and soon swans and crowns and all sorts of linen origami cover the space.

"Dad was devastated. He felt he'd failed, failed us so badly he couldn't ever fix it, couldn't see how he could face us, day after day. So, he didn't. He left. I begged him to stay. We were so close when I was growing up. But I wasn't enough. He couldn't see past losing all that money, couldn't see what he had left. Couldn't see us. *Me*. And when he was gone, Mom crawled into a bottle and never came out."

And just like that, her life was over. She doesn't have to tell me the rest. I can see it on her face. The disappointment, the resignation, the determination to make the best of a bad job. She'd have had to go out and find a job straight away. All kudos to her that she managed to at least get into her chosen field, if not at the level she wanted. I'm sure she'd thought she could work her way up. It must have been crushing to discover, after all that, that she'd never go anywhere. Running every day just to stand still.

My billions have protected me from that. I work because I want to. She was trapped, stuck on the treadmill whether she liked it or not.

I reach out and take her hand in mine. I can see she's close to falling apart, holding herself together with frayed threads of steel and desperate, flickering hope. She lets me take her hand, and it feels like a gift, that she'll let herself lean on me, even a tiny bit, considering her feelings about wealthy men in sharp suits.

It's only her hand in mine, but it feels like a victory.

She sighs, her body relaxing as I stroke my thumb over the inside of her wrist, and for just a moment, she looks at peace.

Then her eyes flick open, and I'm mesmerized, as ever, by their cool green depths. "Can't we just go to another gallery?"

I blink, confused by the sudden change in topic. "I'm sorry?"

"For the auction. There must be any number of high-end galleries in this city. Can't we just approach someone else?"

Right. The auction. For the gala in just under three weeks. Her ability to get back on track after a setback is awe-inspiring. I drag my brain back to the subject in hand, a difficult proposition when her skin is so soft and smooth under my fingers.

"It's not about the price. We're not looking for expensive, we're looking for quirky, different, out of the ordinary. The foundation doesn't just support the poor, it also supports children who have talents which don't fit in traditional academia. We wanted artworks which would fit with that, and they can be hard to find."

Her head tilts slightly, and she looks at me as if we've only just met. Her appraisal continues for long enough to make me slightly uncomfortable, and then her face clears. "I have an idea."

She pulls out her phone and types something in. "One of my friends managed to follow her art after school. She's got a bunch of things I think you'll like."

She hands me her phone, and I'm astonished to see exactly the kind of thing we want. Exuberant, unusual, bursting with life. Whoever this woman is, she's incredibly talented, and exactly what we want. I tell Shay so, and she beams at me.

This time I bask in that smile, knowing I earned it.

She dials a number. "Hi Fiona, it's Shay. I'm well, thanks, how are you?... Awesome! That's great news! Look, I'm organizing an event, and they want to do a silent auction, but with quirky, different stuff, and they love yours... Well, obviously. You're brilliant... Shut up, you're amazing. Anyway, it's on June 21st. Can you make that?... Hmmm, okay, that should be fine. Let me call around and get you some help. I'll call you back in an hour or so, okay?"

She hangs up and looks over at me. "She's got the pieces, but transport might be a problem. This is probably a stupid question, but—"

"We can afford it. Do whatever you need to do." And again, with the smile. I'm on a roll.

I sit back and watch her shine as she makes call after call, wheedling, begging, persuading. People across this city are happy to help her out. That's not just good business relationships. That's being the kind of person people want to help. She's never arrogant or demanding. She just asks, and they say yes.

And why wouldn't they? She's kind and generous and appreciative. She saw an opportunity for her friend, and she's passing it on. Organized and thoughtful on top of everything else.

She's perfect. The kind of woman you want to hold onto always.

The thought rocks me, and yet, it feels so right. My mind starts spinning. I have more than a gala to organize. I need to figure out how to persuade Shay to give me, us, a shot at forever.

***

Shay

Max has been dropping me home in his town car every day, which I both adore and hate. Adore because it's wonderful not to have to fight my way out of the city on the subway, especially in the mid-summer heat and humidity. Hate because it means yet more time in the back of his insanely plush, air-conditioned car, in the dark, just inches from his hard, muscled body, the scent of his cologne teasing me…

Brett must think I'm a nutcase. Every time he opens the door, I'm out of that car like I've been fired from a cannon. It's becoming harder and harder to keep my hands to myself, especially when Max just sits there, looking at me like a lion eyeing up a gazelle.

Not that I'm built like a gazelle, you understand. More like the StayPuft Marshmallow Man, but that doesn't seem to bother Max. If anything, I feel like a queen, a curvy melting queen, when he looks at me that way. The man is a god, and he looks at me like I'm his goddess.

Today, though, the car pulls up a lot sooner than usual, and I look around in confusion. I don't recognize the view out the window, and turn to frown at Max. "Where are we?"

He smiles, but his eyes are hot and hard, roving my body in a way that makes me want to peel my clothes off my suddenly too tight skin.

"I thought a celebration was in order," he says, his voice deeper and rougher than usual. "The project is going extremely well, and you keep forgetting to eat. This way, I can cover both bases."

The door opens, and I look up at the glittering facade of the Shelby Tower, the tallest building in the city. It's home to a lot of things, including a very up market hotel. I look at him. Is he planning to seduce me?

My lady parts suddenly sit up and start to beg. *Oh please, please, please…!* I try to slap them down, but it's no good. I've gone from zero to tingles in the space of a breath.

"It's just dinner, Shay," he says, quietly, and I look back to see the heat banked in his eyes. "It's just dinner."

I drag in a shaky breath and climb out of the car, telling myself I'm not disappointed. I can't sleep with my boss, I just can't...

He puts his hand in the small of my back, guiding me through the revolving doors, and the heat from his skin burns me through my jacket and blouse, sending molten heat trickling through my veins. I focus on the floor, the walls, the inside of the elevator with smooth walls which he doesn't push me up against, and then the doors open...to the night sky.

"Oh!" I can't help it; my gasp of surprise just slips out. This high up, you can actually see stars, since we're so much higher than all the other buildings pumping out light. An inky blanket punctuated with pinpricks of light flows overhead, and I just want to stand there and drink it in until the sun rises.

"Shay, I brought you here to eat, not get a crick in your neck." His hand is at my elbow now, gently but firmly propelling me forwards. Eventually, I accept that I have to look where I'm going, or I'm going to walk into something or trip over, and then I'll just feel stupid.

I hate feeling stupid.

We round a corner to find a small table laid for two, with candles flickering in hurricane lamps, flatware and cutlery gleaming in the light of the flames. Music trickles through the air, a delicate lilting melody, and a waiter stands off to the side, a snowy white napkin draped over one arm. A warming trolley sits next to him, various dishes covered up against the cool night air and whatever bugs might be flying around.

Then I catch a faint waft of citronella and realize they've put bug-repelling candles around. I'm instantly grateful. I'm the kind of person who always gets eaten alive, but now I can relax and enjoy myself.

The waiter steps forward to pull out my chair, but suddenly cringes and backs away. I look around just in time to see a ferocious glare on Max's face before he relaxes and pulls my chair out for me. I can't help giggling and sit, then shiver as his breath brushes my ear.

"I refuse to let any other man this close to you."

He sits down opposite me, and the waiter waits for his signal before approaching with wine. Once our glasses are full, he backs away.

"Honestly, Max, the poor man's terrified. Possessive much?"

Something about the look on his face makes my pussy quiver, moisture pooling between my thighs, and I swallow and rub them together, trying to ease the growing ache between them.

He doesn't say anything, and I decide to shut my mouth. I'm not helping the situation. Besides, I'm starving, and the food smells luscious.

Forty minutes later, I sit back in my chair, sighing happily. "That was amazing. How did you get them to do this?"

The corner of his mouth curves upwards. "It wasn't hard. It's a known private dining space. I asked if it was booked, they said no."

He shrugs, like it was nothing, but it doesn't feel like nothing.

I look around at the candles, the sky above, the cool night breeze teasing my hair. It reminds me of happier times.

"Do tell," says Max, and I realize I spoke out loud.

I don't intend to tell him much, but once I start talking, I can't stop.

"You know how most kids have their birthday parties at Chuck E Cheese or wherever? My dad always used to insist we celebrate my birthdays at home. We'd all be in the garden, and he'd string up lights and bunting and get us all sparklers. My birthday's in October, so it usually got dark about halfway through, so we'd have torches and play Hide And Go Seek and tell scary stories around a bonfire." I smile at the memory and sip my wine.

It's nice to remember the good times with my dad. I'd almost forgotten there were any. "It always seemed like a lot of work, though, and I'd always say I was happy to have a party somewhere else if he didn't want to go to all that trouble. And every time he would just say that nature was way more beautiful than the inside of any building, and it was a pity to waste it."

I swallow, remembering how I'd been planning to come home from college for my birthday, because Dad had insisted I be home for it, just like I always used to be. And then he was the one who wasn't there.

"He gave me this pen," I tell Max, reaching into my purse and pulling out the blue glass pen I use every day for work. "I nearly threw it out after he left, but I couldn't find it. Eventually, I forgave him, and then the pen just showed up one day. Now I'm glad I have it. It's all I have left of him. In the end, everything else had to be sold."

The scrape of a chair snaps me back to the present moment, and I watch Max stand and walk around the table, holding out his hand. I take it, wondering what's happening, then gasp in surprise as he pulls me into his arms and starts moving to the music floating across the empty terrace.

"Relax, Shay. This is meant to be fun, remember?"

His face is so close, and because of our height difference, I have to tip my head back to see his eyes. Being here, in his arms, it feels like a world away from the fear and insecurity that have surrounded me since my dad left. I never realized how much we relied on him for stability, me and my mom, until he wasn't there anymore. Maybe if I'd been more appreciative —

"Stop that."

I frown up at Max. "Stop what?" *Is he a mind reader?*

"Whatever you were thinking about. This isn't the place for unhappy memories. This is a new memory. A good one, I hope."

I smile and relax, giving myself over to the movement of his body and the firm embrace of his arms. "Very good ones," I murmur.

A faint click echoes somewhere behind me, and when I look around, I see the waiter has gone. I look up at Max. I know what he wants. I want the same thing. But right now, I'm content to just move to the music, safe against his chest, his firm grip leading me where I need to go.

The music ends, and I move to step back, but instead, he pulls me in closer, his hands sliding up my arms, over my shoulders and into my hair, cupping my jaw, angling my head. My lips part in anticipation of his kiss, but he merely stands there, watching me. I lick my lips, starting to get nervous under his unwavering stare.

"What?" I whisper, finally, when I can't take the suspense anymore.

He shakes his head. "You're perfect. I'm so glad I found you."

And then his head descends, and his mouth covers mine, warm and firm and demanding.

Heat unfurls inside me, lapping lazily at my skin, slithering down my spine to coil in my belly. I moan, leaning into him, and he pulls me closer, his tongue sliding between my lips to dominate my mouth. I cling to him, my hands clutching at his arms, his shoulders, before finally wrapping around the back of his neck and hanging on tight, my anchor in the storm he's unleashing inside me.

He walks me backwards. I try to look where I'm going, but he refuses to break the kiss, his hands imprisoning me so that I have no option but to trust him, that he won't let me trip, let me fall.

That he won't let go.

A door opens and closes, and the night breeze is cut off. Then a soft rush of air envelops me, and he allows me to lift my head and look around.

We're in a huge apartment, tastefully decorated in pale blues and greys, a relaxing color scheme enhanced with the occasional pop of red or purple. In front of me is a vast lounge, with a kitchen on the far side separated from the lounge by an enormous island, complete with stove, double sink, and breakfast bar.

"Wow."

"Now look to your right," he murmurs in my ear, and I shiver at his hot breath on my sensitive skin. The shiver goes right down my spine, making my pussy quiver, and it takes all my strength to do as I'm told and look to my right.

The biggest bed I've ever seen stands there, at least seven feet across. The sheets are a rich dark red, but I'm grateful to notice they're not satin. It would look too much like a bordello, or at least, my idea of a bordello, not that I've ever been in one.

Then I realize what's about to happen, and I tremble for a different reason. I swallow, licking lips suddenly gone dry, and freeze. What do I do? I have no idea how to act in this situation, and this isn't even a normal situation. At least, I'm assuming most people don't hook up with their boss.

Oh shit, he's my boss. What am I thinking? I shouldn't even be considering this —

"You're thinking too hard," he says, snapping me out of my whirling thoughts and making me jump. He eases my jacket off my shoulders, and I hesitate, then let it go. I mean, we've come this far, I kind of have to go ahead with it, right?

Liar, says the little voice deep inside. *You know you want this. Stop lying to yourself.*

I hang my head, just a little, then jump again as two cool fingers slide under my chin, lifting my head so that our eyes meet.

"What's going on inside that busy head, Shay? We don't have to do this, you know."

"We don't?" I stare up at him. "Then why..." It seems like a stupid question to ask why he brought me here, when there's this huge bed right there, but still. I'm confused.

His jaw clenches. "You need to associate with a higher class of individual," he says, his voice rough with anger. "We're here because I want you, and I'm a hundred and ten percent sure you want me, but we're not going to do a damn thing until you're ready to do it. And that's because you are now associating with a higher class of individual. Congratulations."

A startled laugh bursts from my mouth, and his eyes are drawn immediately to my lips, making me lick them again with nerves.

"The thing is..." God, how do I say this? It's ridiculous, surely. A twenty-four-year-old virgin? How is that even possible? I look up at him and see no judgment, no frustration that I'm making him wait. If anything, he seems content just to watch me, just to be near me, one hand at my waist, his palm burning me through my shirt, the other at my throat, stroking my pulse with his thumb, making me shiver.

"The thing is?" he prompts.

"Right." I take a deep breath. "I'm a virgin."

His eyes widen for a moment, and I'm sure I've blown it. What man this powerful, this experienced, would want someone who didn't know the first thing about sex? I look away, tears pricking at my eyes. Not good enough. Once again, I'm not good enough.

Then his hand tightens, just a little around my throat, and I can't stop the bolt of lust which shoots through me, straight to my pussy, lighting it on fire. My eyes jerk up to meet his, and the heat I see there makes me realize I've got it all wrong.

His hand slides further around my waist, drawing me closer to him. He turns and presses me against the wall, his hard, solid muscle imprinting itself on my soft curves so that I can feel every inch of him, including all the very hard inches below his waist, pressing into my belly.

I twist against him as tension gathers between my thighs, my head falling back against the wall as his lips skate over my throat. Then he nips at my skin, and I yelp, gasping as the pain sends electricity into my blood, making me burn with need.

"Do you want me to be your first?" He murmurs in my ear, his voice rough as freshly laid concrete. "Do you want me in you, making you scream with pleasure, giving you your first orgasms on a man's cock?"

"Oh God, *yes*," I gasp, barely able to speak through the images his words send cascading through my mind.

"Look at me, Shay," he orders, lifting his head, and I moan at the loss of the heat of his lips, the delicious friction of his tongue and teeth. "Look at me and tell me you want me, you want this."

I lever my eyes open and stare at him. His hair is a mess where I've been running my hands through it without even realizing. His eyes are wild, and yet there's a stillness about him. He's truly waiting for me to say stop or go. All this time, I thought he was the one with the power, and now I suddenly realize, it was in my hands all along.

"I want you," I tell him. "I want this, with you." *Forever*, adds the little voice inside, and I bite my tongue before it slips out. It's only been a few days. It's too soon for that kind of thinking.

Is it? asks that little voice.

As his lips crash down on mine and I give myself up to the heat and power of them, I push the thought away and give myself up to sensation.

He pulls my hands off his shoulders and pins them above my head, making me squirm with the thrill of being restrained. How does he know exactly how to light me up? His other hand settles at the base of my throat, and just like that, I don't care. I just want to focus on the slide of his hand, gliding slowly, oh so slowly, down to the collar of my blouse.

His fingers slide the button free, without touching my skin, the lack of contact making my chest tighten in anticipation. Then he frees the next and the next, until he pulls the fabric free of my skirt and pushes it aside, bearing my heaving breasts, my skin prickling with need, desperate for his touch.

"You are perfect," he mutters, his voice hoarse. "Don't ever believe you're not." He lowers his head, and I moan as his lips drag over the upper swells of my breasts, making my heart race and my breath catch as heat and light skitter through my veins. I can't control the movement of my hips, my breasts, as I strain to get closer to him, and then his tongue sweeps over my skin, and I give a strangled cry.

Slick heat massages my flesh, punctuated with tiny nips of his teeth, the combination making me moan, then beg for more.

"Your wish is my command," he murmurs silkily, before reaching around me to unhook my bra and pushing it aside to close his mouth around one aching, swollen nipple.

My head falls back against the wall. I can't think, I can't speak except to plead for more, for everything. The pressure of his body against mine is the only thing holding me up. My legs shake uncontrollably as sensation floods my body before drawing down into my pussy in an lava-hot ball of pulsing need.

He tortures my breasts well beyond the point where I think I can handle it, writhing against him in desperation as he worships my flesh with his mouth and hand. He lifts his head and stares at me, his eyes so dark they're black, and I can only gasp and pant, my body one long, vibrating curve of need.

He smiles, a self-satisfied smile which would make me want to slap him if I wasn't on the point of melting into a puddle, then lifts me away from the wall, sliding my shirt off my shoulders and down my arms, before sweeping me into his arms and carrying me to the bed.

The sheets are cool against my back, and I stare at him as he pulls my bra away, then takes off my shoes. His hands skim up my legs, and I quiver as my over-sensitized skin thrills to his touch. Moving to my hip, he slides the zipper of my skirt down, down, down, then hooks his fingers into the waistband and eases it off me, and I'm just able to lift my ass to help.

Lying there, naked except for my panties, cool air washing over me, I can't help but register the heat in his eyes as they rove over my body. Finally, I can take his inspection no longer and draw my legs up, wanting to hide my exceptionally generous curves from him. He's still completely dressed, and it makes me feel even more naked.

"No," he says, and I freeze. "Don't ever hide from me. You are beautiful."

He prowls up the bed, his tie brushing over the soft skin of my thigh, my belly, my chest, and he kisses me. This isn't like before. This isn't conquest.

This is worship. Adoration.

I feel *adored*.

His lips and tongue are gentle on mine, coaxing instead of demanding, and when I open up for him, he remains gentle, but firm, controlling me so carefully, as if I might break. I delve my hands into his hair, glorying in the cool silky texture of the strands running between my fingers, my legs lifting to curve around his hips as his weight settles over mine. I gasp into his mouth as his erection nudges my core through his pants, sliding over my clit, sending a wave of sensation crashing through me, and he raises his head and smiles.

I smile back, but only a little. He looks predatory, like a shark, like he wants to eat me, and then he's drawing my hands out of his hair again and pressing them against the headboard. A moment later there's a click, and another, and when he lets go, my wrists are held fast in velvet-lined cuffs.

My eyes widen, and my heart beats faster. He grins, now every bit the conqueror, as he moves over my throat, my breasts, my belly and my thighs. His mouth and his hands, now free to roam as I squirm and writhe beneath him, take their time in learning me. Every dip, every curve, every sensitive place is thoroughly explored. I'm helpless to resist this torture, even as my skin grows tighter and my pussy aches with need, my legs trembling and my breath locking in my throat with every touch.

His fingers flirt with the waistband of my panties, and every touch makes me more desperate, whimpering as his fingertips brush over my heated skin. He draws the fabric down my legs, then runs his hands up the insides of my legs, bending them and placing the soles of my feet flat on the bed, baring my dripping pussy to his avid gaze.

My core clenches and releases, desperate for something, for more, aching and needy, and when his tongue slides over my pussy and my clit in one long stroke, I arch off the bed, crying out at the pleasure crashing through me. He throws his arms over my hips, pinning me down, helpless to resist or avoid what he's doing to me. His tongue slides inside me, making me squeal at the slickness and heat, a sensation I never imagined before now. Then his mouth closes over my clit and *sucks*, and I explode, screaming and gasping as my orgasm rolls on and on, seizing me in an iron grip over and over, until finally I lie there, limp and trembling in his arms.

He raises his head, then moves up my body to kiss me, and I taste myself on his tongue. I'm still searching for air when he stands and pulls off his clothes, and the sight of all that hard, golden muscle causes a fresh rush of moisture to my aching pussy.

"See something you like?" he asks, and I blush, but I can't tear my eyes away. Then he takes off his pants and underwear, and my eyes widen at his cock is revealed.

It's beautiful, bold, strong and *enormous*. How the fuck is that going to fit inside me?

He approaches the bed, his big hands strong and sure and kind as he skims a palm over my breast, making me quiver. "Don't worry. By the time I slip inside you, you'll be so wet, all you'll feel is pleasure."

He rolls my nipple between his fingers, making me gasp, then settles his solid muscular body between my legs. I brace myself, but he just smiles and lowers his mouth to my nipple, taking it between his teeth and flicking it lightly with his tongue. I'm still moaning at the exquisite sensation when I feel the hard rod of his cock slide over my pussy and back down again. Slick with my juices, it presses over my clit as it passes, making me cry out at the sharp bolt of pleasure arrowing through me.

He kisses my breasts, my neck, nipping at my skin as his cock slides back and forth over my pussy and clit. I'm shrieking with every breath, desperate for more but too far gone to ask for it. The tension is a living thing inside me, coiling and writhing in my pussy, drawing me in tighter and tighter, until suddenly he pulls back and slides his huge cock straight into my desperate, needy channel, and as he slams home, my orgasm rips through me, breaking me apart into a thousand pieces of glass, all lit with sunlight and falling through an endless sky.

And he doesn't stop moving, even as I scream and plead and tug on the cuffs binding me to the bed. His hips pump and slide, his mouth skimming my breasts, my throat, my lips, his tongue flicking against mine as I beg for mercy. He doesn't move faster or slower, simply maintains the same punishing rhythm, and my legs wrap around him, my hips seeking the edge once more, my breath coming in ragged gasps, until the tension draws in again, pulling me deeper and tighter, harder and higher, until finally, I break yet again, and fly apart into endless pieces of pleasure, scattered like hummingbirds in a storm, and he roars with triumph as he follows me over the cliff.

We lie there for a moment, gasping for breath.

"Did I hurt you?" he says. "I'm sorry. I wasn't gentle."

I can't help laughing, although it's little more than a sigh as that's all I have the energy for. "You didn't...hurt me... It was...great...perfect."

He pulls out and I groan at the friction of his cock sliding free. Then he gathers me into his arms and carries me into the bathroom. He fills the bath and turns on the jet, then gets in, still cradling me against his chest, and I fall asleep with his heartbeat thudding powerfully against my ear.

***

Max

I eye my reflection in the mirror, shaking my head at the ridiculous smile on my face. Everyone I meet today is going to think I'm on drugs if I can't wipe this goofy expression off my face, but I can't bring myself to care. It's been several days now since I took Shay out to dinner, and then feasted in an entirely different way. I wish I'd been able to repeat the experience, but the closer we get to the day of the gala, the more and more details turn up needing attention, and I'm well aware of how exhausted Shay was the day after I took her virginity. She covered it well, but I know her by now, and I know when she's not at her best.

I'm still in awe of her trust in me, and I refuse to cheapen her first experience by insisting on it again and again when she clearly needs her rest. Besides, she's holding up her end of the bargain like a champ. She's working even harder, as though trying to convince both of us that she was never in this job to score a man, as though I need convincing of that.

She's as honest as the day is long, and that's only one of the many things I appreciate about her. She's the best assistant I've ever had, somehow managing to field most of my phone calls as well as dealing with the gala. She's also the sweetest, smartest, sexiest woman I've ever met.

At this point, I realize I've been standing here, staring into space, daydreaming about Shay instead of tying my tie. I pull it apart and start again, forcing myself to focus until the job is done. I'm just looking forward to the gala being over so that I can take her out on a proper date. For all the time we've been spending together, we've only been on one date, and I intend to wine and dine her to the extreme, take her all the places she's always wanted to go. I won't let her down the way her father did.

Most of all, I'm looking forward to taking her out, and then keeping her in the whole of the next day, naked and sated in my bed.

My phone rings, yanking me out of a sweet and very hot memory, and I snatch it up and stab at the screen.

"What?" I snarl. All I have of Shay's body right now are memories. I don't appreciate having them interrupted.

"Max, buddy, you need to switch to decaf. It's too early for you to be this uptight."

I sigh. Of course, it would be Leo, one of my oldest friends, calling me up at stupid o'clock on a Wednesday morning. "What do you want, slacker?"

"A woman, a beer, and a king-size bed, not in that order. Anyway, who are you calling slacker? I hear you're running around town organizing a party instead of doing your work."

I snort. "This from the man who literally spends his life going to parties."

"Really boring parties. Please tell me yours is different."

"I booked forty-eight pole dancers, just for you. They've got this great routine where they tie themselves to pillars and you get to untie them. But you can only use your teeth."

"I am all over that."

I shake my head. "Yeah, and my mother would have a coronary. You know the venue, right? You coming?"

"Of course. And your mother can handle plenty. At least, that's what she told me the oth—"

"Jesus, Leo." I hang up on his laughter and pull on my jacket. I'll be seeing Shay in about twenty minutes, and my day is already looking bright.

Shay looks as beautiful as ever when I arrive at the office, even in the plain clothes she insists on wearing. Then I want to rap my head against the wall. Of course, her clothes are cheap and boring and don't do her justice. She probably can't afford anything nicer. I pull out my wallet and hand her a credit card.

"What's this for?" she asks. "The vendors are all sending invoices to the foundation. Oh shit, that is what they're supposed to be doing, right?"

For a moment she looks utterly panicked, and it's adorable how she thinks she could possibly do anything wrong.

"Yes, that's exactly what they're supposed to be doing. This is for you."

She frowns at it. "Why do I need a credit card?"

"To get some clothes."

She looks taken aback, and I have to remind myself that she never intended to snag a rich boyfriend. She has no idea of the benefits now available to her.

"Go shopping, get some nice things. And pick up something extra pretty for the gala. You want to look special."

Not that even the most exquisite of gowns will do anything but make her look even more stunning, but I don't care. I want the world to know she's mine, that I intend to put her on a pedestal for everyone to bow down to. She deserves the best of everything, and I'm determined to make it happen. I know she's been getting by on a shoestring until now, having had to care for her mom and pay medical bills, but she doesn't need to do that anymore. I'm going to take care of her, and this is just the start.

***

Shay

And just like that, I'm insecure again. He hates my clothes? Well, that's a pity because I like my clothes. I bought them with my own money, dammit. They may not be haute couture, (okay, let's be honest, they're all superstore own brand stuff), but they fit, mostly, and I bought them myself. I don't need a man to clothe me. Does he think this was all just about scoring a clothing allowance?

I force myself to stay calm and put the card in my wallet before heading into the front office to meet yet another vendor. I'm not going to make a scene here. There are too many people around, and

I have a professional reputation to maintain, especially if Max thinks I'm just his doll to dress as he pleases.

I'm probably overreacting, right? I mean, in these circles people really are judged based on their appearance. I've always done my best to look professional with the budget I had to work with, but Hennessy had a uniform, and I haven't had a chance to buy anything nicer since starting with Max. Every waking minute involves talking to people, meeting other people, and visiting suppliers in order to hash out last minute details.

A moment later, a terrible thought occurs to me. What if he's actually embarrassed by my clothes? After all, his suits cost at least what I make in a month, and that's at the insanely high salary he's paying me for this job. Then I nearly drop the very expensive crystal vase I'm looking at when I wonder if that insanely high salary was always just for this job, or whether he'd always planned to get me into bed. Was it just an advance payment for services rendered?

I put the vase down, much to the relief of the woman who brought them in for me to look at, and try to get a handle on my panicked thoughts. Am I just an employee? Just one more woman to bang? When this job is over, will Max's interest in me evaporate too?

I shake my head. I can't let myself wallow in all this uncertainty. I'll talk to him about it later, but for now, I have a job to do. And it does not include buying clothes. I can't go spending his money like that, especially when the job will be over in less than ten days' time. Particularly if I'm just a temporary fling for him. The last thing I'll want is gorgeous clothes bought with his credit card because he was embarrassed to be seen with me in my usual suits.

My phone rings, a welcome distraction from my spiraling thoughts, and I check the caller ID. It's the venue, and I shake off the feeling of impending doom, even as a hard lump settles in my chest. "Shay Thorne."

"Ms. Thorne, uh, I'm so sorry to have to tell you this…"

I stare at the phone, then put it back to my ear. I'm hearing what he's saying but the words don't make sense. They can't, because if they did… "How much water?"

My question cuts across the manager's panicked babbling. He sighs. "A lot. About six hundred thousand gallons."

I drag in a breath, let it out. Draw in another. Nope, I'm still paralyzed. "H-How long will it take to fix?"

Across the room, Max lifts his head. I don't want to look at him right now, I don't want to look at anything. If I focus on anything at all, then the world will be real, what the manager of the venue is telling me will be real and then…

"Longer than ten days."

"How long?" I bite out.

"The assessor says…approximately three months."

My jaw starts to quiver, and I make my goodbyes as quickly as possible. I will not cry at the poor man. It's not his fault that the hotel's water system developed a fault and voided the entire contents of the water tank straight through the ceiling of the ballroom where we're supposed to be holding the most prestigious event of the year in just over a week. The same ballroom which was already partly decorated for the event.

"Shay?"

Max's voice is quiet, gentle, and it brings tears to my eyes. Tears I force back because, dammit, I'm a professional. I buy my own clothes, and I solve my own problems, and in this case, that includes assessing the damage to the venue and all the gear we had in there preparatory to the event.

"We need to get over to the venue. Now."

He checks his watch. "We do. I'm meeting Nash there in fifteen minutes to go over security details."

I bark out a laugh. He looks startled, and I finally feel able to explain the problem. His jaw clenches and then he stands and strides over to the door, pulling his phone from his pocket as he goes to call Brett. He opens the door and looks back at me expectantly, and I grab my jacket and the binder and scurry after him.

I tell myself all the way over that maybe it's not that bad. Maybe it's salvageable. Maybe maybe maybe…

Standing in the ruins of the ballroom, it's abundantly clear that it's not salvageable. Most of the hardware can be cleaned up, but most of the room itself is still six inches deep in water. They're pumping it out, but it's going to take weeks to dry out, and then they'll need to assess the fabric of the room, make sure paneling isn't rotting in the walls before they can even think about re-plastering.

"We need a new venue," I sigh.

"No shit," mutters Nash. He's a big guy and scary as hell. I'm kind of relieved to see him showing emotion, but the fact that he is just shows what a total fucking disaster we're looking at.

I look over at Max, whose face could be carved from marble for all the expression he's showing. I have no idea what he's thinking and that worries me. Seeing him closed up like that makes me wonder what he's hiding. "I guess I'll go and talk to the manager?"

He lifts an eyebrow at me. "Go. Do your job."

Normally I wouldn't think twice about such a comment. I'd probably see it as a compliment, an indication of how highly he thinks of my ability to do my job that he doesn't even feel the need to offer guidance or accompany me. But now I find myself wondering if it's just a reminder that I'm only an employee.

I step away, trying to get a signal on my phone. The building is so huge, it's quicker to call him than to wander around looking for him. The phone rings. And rings. I'm guessing the manager's on a call and wait for it to go to voicemail so I can leave a message.

"That's your assistant?" asks Nash, behind me. He sounds admiring, which is nice. I can use the moral support.

"Not for much longer," says Max, and I freeze.

"Why not?"

"Look at her. Some things just aren't meant to be."

He sounds so dismissive, so cold, so it's only fitting that I'm feeling cold, too. Ice settles over my skin, prickling through to chill my blood, my bones, my heart.

I was right. I'm not good enough. I was never going to be. How could I, with my lack of degree and crappy, cheap clothes and shitty family with terrible business sense? Had I actually kidded myself, even for a minute, a *second* that I would ever be good enough for him? For my boss? My *billionaire* boss?

I'm horribly, chillingly aware of just how stupid I've been, and when I find myself walking across the room, away from him, away from my stupidity, I don't even want to stop. I don't want to turn around. I don't want to scream at him. I can't face him, can't stand to see that dismissal on his face.

It was bad enough when the cops told Dad that his money was gone, and they couldn't get it back. It was worse when he walked out, even as I stood there and begged him not to go. I wasn't enough then, and I'm not enough now. I'll never be enough.

I keep on walking, down the corridor, across the lobby, and right out of the building onto the busy street. I don't know where I'm going, but it doesn't matter. All that's really important is that I'm walking away from yet another failure. I pull out my phone and type a quick email to my now former boss, tendering my immediate resignation and accepting the loss of my last paycheck in lieu of notice.

Somehow, I make it home, and then I cry until I run out of tears.

***

Max

I sit in my office staring at the far wall. Her desk is still there, littered with papers and pens and washi tape and God knows what other magical ingredients she felt were necessary to do her job. I turn her blue pen over in my fingers. I should have given it back to her before now, but she won't respond to emails or calls. I'd go over to her place, but it's pretty clear she doesn't want to see me.

It's been a week since she quit, and I haven't been able to bring myself to clear the stuff away. Somewhere, deep down, I know it's because I'm hoping she'll come back, that she'll walk through that door and everything will be okay again.

Because it sure as hell isn't okay now. We still don't have a venue for the gala, and I know I should be working on it, finding us a place to go, but I cannot locate even a single fuck to give. Not without Shay. Not without seeing her and talking to her and seeing her smile and hearing her laugh and —

My phone rings, and I snarl my name down the line without checking caller ID. I don't even care who it is. Shay left, and I don't know why. I'm pissed as hell, and I miss her like crazy. If she walked back in right now, I'd shake her until her teeth rattled, and then I'd kiss her until her knees buckled, and then I'd —

"Max. We talked about the caffeine, man."

"Fuck off, Leo What is it?

There's a brief silence. I know I've pissed him off, but I'm too lost to care. Nothing matters anymore. Not without her.

"I heard about the water issue. Have you got a new venue yet?"

"Nope."

More silence. Finally, he sighs. "What's going on, buddy?"

"It doesn't concern you."

"Fuck that, and fuck you, Lupin. You know it concerns me. Now pull that stick out of your ass and level with me."

I drop my head to my desk and rap it against the wood a few times. He doesn't hang up, but neither do I.

"Shay quit," I finally admit. "And she seems to have left me too."

"Well, I'm not surprised," he says, easily. "I mean, I heard you were about to fire her. Women have an instinct for that kind of thing. And what is it with you and assistants, anyway?"

"Hey, Shay's the first one I ever— wait, what?" I stare at my phone, speechless with confusion. Finally, I find my words again. "What the *fuck* are you talking about? I wasn't going to fire her!"

"You said she wasn't going to be your assistant anymore."

"Nash has a big fucking mouth. And I wasn't going to fire her. She's an organizational genius and clearly meant to be organizing huge parties on a regular basis, and I don't usually even throw one a year. That's Mom's thing. Shay'll probably be beating off job offers with a bat after the gala. If we can find a fucking venue. Everything else is on rails. She did in two weeks what Cherise couldn't do in eight months."

"Huh. Well, let's face it, Cherise had other priorities."

I grunt. He's not wrong there.

"So, when you were acting like your thing with her was just temporary," he continues. "Was that just you being a dumbass?"

"It's not temporary," I snap. "At least, I didn't want it to be."

"Like I said, women have an instinct for that kind of thing. I'm guessing you didn't actually say anything about wanting a long-term deal."

I'm pissed that he called it so easily. Am I really that predictable? "How do you know?"

He snorts. "I've known you a long time, man. Let's call it a wild guess."

"If she thought I was about to kick her to the curb, why didn't she say something?"

"She did. She said, 'I quit.'"

"You know what I mean."

"I don't know, man. You know her better than I do. Anyway, give me a call when you have a new venue. You know I'm there for you."

He ends the call, and I frown at nothing, trying to figure out where I went wrong. At what point did I give her the impression that I didn't want her around?

Then I remember her relaxing into my arms on the roof terrace that night, the things she told me, and I want to kick my own ass. Her dad left her, and then her mom pretty much did the same. They forced her to stand alone, to always be ready to take care of herself. She'd just begun to trust that I wouldn't walk away from her, but she was still primed to think she was about to be abandoned all over again. It doesn't even matter what I said, what I did. It's what I didn't say. *Be mine. Stay with me. Be with me forever.*

I lean back in my chair and give a frustrated groan. Damn, I fucked this up bad. And I let the gala go to shit because I've spent the last week wallowing in my own emotional sewage.

"Dammit, Leo," I snarl at the wall. "Couldn't you have called sooner?"

I look at her desk, remembering her face when she talked about her dad always throwing her parties in the garden, how dedicated he was to making them as beautiful as possible.

Suddenly it's like someone turned on a light and I slap my forehead, then grab my phone. I'm about to dial Shay, but I change my mind and call Brett instead. Some things are best done in person.

***

Shay

I sit on my couch, staring at the computer screen. I've spent the last week wallowing and eating way too much ice cream, and today, I decided I needed to just pull on my big girl panties and find another job. Unfortunately, all I can think about is Max. How he treated me, how he looked at me when I was lying naked on that bed.

Did I get it wrong? Should I have waited, tried to understand why he was letting me go? More to the point, how did I misread him so badly? I always thought I was a pretty good judge of character, but I got him so wrong. Which makes me wonder if I did get him wrong. Maybe he is a good guy, and I just...got the wrong end of the stick?

But I don't know how to interpret 'she's not going to be around much longer' any other way than 'I'm not interested in her anymore'. That seems pretty clear cut to me, and yet...

And yet...

I shake my head. It's done. I quit, and without a notice period too. That's not going to make it easy to find another gig, especially when the Lupin gala goes ahead without me, even though I did most of the work. I walked out on Max at the worst possible time, right when he needed a new venue. Even if I did misunderstand, he's never going to forgive me for that. I just torpedoed my career as well as walking away from a shitty not-actually-a-relationship.

I hope. Cos if I was wrong about that too… Well, how many really important things can you truly fuck up beyond redemption in a single day?

I refocus on the screen, then jump as the buzzer goes. I frown and stare at it. No one comes to my apartment, except for delivery guys, and I haven't ordered in. Which I probably should because living on ice cream isn't healthy, even by my standards.

The buzzer goes again, and I roll my eyes. Probably someone trying to get into the building because whoever they're after isn't answering. It happens several times a week. It screams again, and this time whoever it is doesn't let up.

"All right, all right," I mutter, dragging myself off the couch and going over to the entry-phone. "What?"

"Are you going to let me in?"

I freeze, that voice sliding right down my spine and curling around my pussy, which immediately starts to throb. "I...I..."

"Let me in, Shay. I need your help."

That gets my attention. Of course, he's not here for me. Not *me*. He needs Events Coordinator Shay, the one who gets things done, works miracles, makes the happy ever after come true.

Except her own.

But I walked out on him. I quit. Why is he here now? Surely he must hate me?

"Are you there?"

"Yes," I yelp, shaking myself and hitting the buzzer to let him in. Either way, I'm going to find out. "Fifth floor. Elevator's out."

I wince as I say it, but it's better than him wasting time standing in the elevator pressing buttons when it's not going anywhere.

I open the front door, and he appears a couple of minutes later, not a hair out of place even though he's just come up five flights of stairs. And he must have run to have got up here so quickly.

He must work out a lot, I think, and then suddenly I remember the body he's packing under his clothes, and I want to slap myself for thinking stupid thoughts. Especially because now I'm thinking about what we did after he ditched the aforementioned clothes, and I'm blushing hard enough to set my hair alight.

I realize I'm just standing there, staring at him, and step aside to let him in.

He stands in the lounge and looks around. I refuse to look around myself and see what a mess the place is. He came here, making me remember things I don't want to remember. He can cope with the squalor.

Which is probably too strong a word, but there are too many empty ice cream cartons in the trash for me to call it tidy.

"What do you want?" I ask him, pleased to note my voice is steady, even though I'm trembling inside. He's bigger than I remember, taller, more built. His hair gleams in the light, and when he looks at me, his eyes flicker for a moment before they turn cool and he's all business.

"I have a solution."

I raise my eyebrows at him. "To what?"

"Our lack of a venue for the biggest event in the city? The one that's supposed to be running in three days' time?"

Oh. That.

"Right," I say. "Congratulations. Why are you here?"

The corner of his mouth twitches, but then he schools his face and I'm sure I must have imagined it. "I need your help to make it happen. There's a lot of things to coordinate. I can't do it alone."

"You haven't hired another coordinator?" I'm horrified, albeit stupidly pleased. He hasn't replaced me, but that begs the question, what's he been doing for the last week without an event coordinator?

"Of course not," he says. "You're the only one I want."

My heart leaps in my chest, and I scowl inwardly. I'm not getting my hopes up. I'm the only *event planner* he wants, that's all he said. It's a compliment, yes. A professional compliment. Nothing to get silly about.

"So, you want to hire me back?" Might as well make sure we're talking about what I think we're talking about.

This time he definitely smiles. "As far as I'm concerned, you never left."

I swallow. I don't deserve that. I walked out on the job and left him with a real mess. If anyone found out, I'd never get hired for another job ever again. I raise my chin. All the more reason to make this one perfect. It'll hurt, working next to him, but I'm a professional. I can gentle along my broken heart for three days. Then I can come home and eat more ice cream.

My stomach growls.

And maybe some real food, too.

"Okay. Where's the new venue?"

"The Lupin Gardens."

"The ones on the family estate?" I gape at him.

"That's the ones. You in?"

The Lupin Gardens are beautifully laid out gardens, with formal and informal areas, surrounding the vast mansion the Lupins call a country home and everyone else calls a goddamn palace. It's the perfect answer. The house is gorgeous, but more to the point, it's close enough for everyone to drive out to the venue and be able to get back to the city the same day. There's more than enough parking as well, so that won't be an issue.

"Can we use the house's staff?"

"Of course." He looks around, then back at me. "Do you need to change, or can we go now?"

Having the staff on hand will be massively helpful, considering there's a million and one things we'll need to do in order to get the place ready in time. I look down at my sweats and baggy shirt with *My unicorn says he's real and I believe him* written across the front.

I know, I know. I said I bought my clothes, and he'd just have to cope, but I have my limits. Even I don't wear pajamas to work.

"Give me five minutes."

I'm back out in three, stepping into my shoes and grabbing the jacket he's holding out for me. "You know, holding the gala at the Lupin Gardens is inspired."

"I know," he says. "By you."

I pause in the act of opening the front door and look back at him. Whatever I'm expecting, I'm taken totally by surprise when he cups my face, slides his hands into my hair, and pulls me in for a very hot kiss, all lips and tongue and slick heat. By the time he releases me, I can barely remember my own name, let alone what I'm supposed to be doing.

He hands me my phone, and I blink at it. It takes me a few seconds to even remember what it is.

"As much as I want to push you up against that wall and make you scream my name," he says, "We have work to do."

And then he smirks as it takes me three attempts to dial the first number because my hands are shaking so much.

***

Shay

It's half past ten on Midsummer's Eve and the Twenty-Fourth Lupin Family Foundation Fundraising Gala is in full swing in the gardens of the Lupin family home. Colored lights play over the Georgian-style stone walls, turning the pale stone into a rainbow. Streamers and LED candles hang everywhere, interspersed with artwork by children supported by the Foundation. The youngest contributor is five, the oldest twenty-five, and the pieces add a personal, human touch to the proceedings. The guests can see exactly what they're raising money for, and I'm sure it's helped loosen a few purse strings just that little bit more. The auction of Fiona's art is over, but some of these pieces, intended only as decoration, have even had interest from potential buyers. I've had great fun taking contact details to pass on to the artists so they can follow up if they wish.

"Thank you, Mrs. Van Reisen. I will pass your details on to Dereese." My planner is filling up with names, email addresses, telephone numbers, and the names of the artwork they want to buy.

"Please do, Ms, Thorne." Shirley Van Reisen's beehive quivers with her enthusiasm. One of the richest people in the country, with independent wealth to match her husband's, she's still adorable in her excitement. "I think this young man has an excellent career ahead of him, and I want to be in on the ground floor!"

She sails away to rejoin the party, stopping to speak with a woman who looks faintly familiar. She points towards me and pats the woman on the shoulder. Piercing blue eyes turn my way, and my stomach tilts.

It's Callie Resnick. She puts on the best events on the whole of the East Coast, the kind of person who charges twice what everyone else does and is still booked a year in advance because she's just that good. Working with her would be my dream, and as she heads toward me, I realize I'm staring at her like she's a particularly juicy steak.

I pull myself together in time to shake her hand like a normal person, still a little star struck.

"Ms. Thorne, I understand? I'm Callie Resnick, of Resnick Events. It's a pleasure to meet you."

"Please believe me when I say the pleasure is all mine," I tell her fervently, and she laughs.

"You've put on quite an event here, and I understand you pulled it off on an insanely tight schedule?"

I'm still a little embarrassed by this. "People keep talking about it like I pulled off a miracle, which I did, but that's my job."

She raises an eyebrow at me. "Do not devalue your work, my dear. You did pull off a miracle, and I need that kind of passion and dedication at my company. Please call me on Monday. I look forward to discussing your future career." She hands me a dark blue business card with her name picked out in silver and flows away towards the dance floor.

I watch her go, then stare down at the card. She's right. I need to stop devaluing myself. I take a moment to hug myself with glee, then look around to see what else needs to be dealt with.

It all seems to be running smoothly. The catering supervisor gives me a thumbs up, then hustles over with a bowl of creme brûlée. "I know you didn't stop to eat, so here, I saved one for you. Caramelized it myself."

She hands me a spoon, then points imperiously at a table. I sit, more than grateful to be off my feet. My shoes are gorgeous, but somewhat unforgiving over the course of the sixteen hours I've been running around in them.

I dig into my dessert and repress a moan of appreciation.

"I've missed that sound," says Max, right next to me, and I almost choke.

"Dear God, don't do that to me!" I thump my chest, trying to dislodge my heart from my throat. "Especially not when I'm eating something this good."

His eyes are dark as I finish the most amazing creme brûlée I've ever eaten. It's hard to concentrate when he looks at me like that. We've barely stopped over the last three days. There hasn't been time for a conversation about anything other than the gala, let alone anything more personal.

But now...

"It's all running well?" he asks. "No disasters?"

I shake my head, barely able to believe it. "Everything's perfect. The auction's over, dinner has been cleared away, and everyone else is taking care of their tools and supplies. I think my work here is done." I sit back with a sigh. I'm happy it has gone so well, but I should be happier, especially with my appointment with Callie Resnick on Monday.

Try as I might, though, I can't help being only too aware that this is the last time I'll see Max. Apart from that one kiss on Tuesday afternoon, he hasn't touched me in any but the most professional manner since stepping back into my life. And why would he? I walked out on the project at the critical moment and still managed to get a shot at my dream job out of it. I don't deserve anything else.

And yet, I miss him. And I'm going to go on missing him. And that...makes me sad.

"So, everything's done. It's finished." His tone is final, but there's something else in it, something dark and soft and...no, I won't get my hopes up like that.

I bite my lip, then nod. "I guess this is goodbye."

His eyes bore into mine, and then he stands up and grabs my hand. "The hell it is."

He tugs me out of my seat and across the terrace, through a set of French doors and into a large room, dominated by a huge desk. He locks the door, then spins me round and presses me up against the wall, his hands in my hair, his erection grinding into my belly as he covers my mouth with his.

I gasp, wrapping my legs around his waist and moaning as his cock nestles right where I want it, hard against my clit, sliding just right. I don't know what's happening, but if this is the last time I get to feel this, I want to enjoy it, embrace it. I'm going to remember every last second.

He slides one hand under my ass, holding me against him as he turns and crosses the room, sitting me down on the desk before reaching beneath my skirt and ripping my panties clean off. I cry out in surprise and arousal, then his hand covers my mouth just as his fingers slide into my pussy, already wet with need. I shriek against his palm, falling back onto the leather surface of the desk, and he rips my blouse open and pushes my bra aside, taking my nipple into his mouth and biting down on it.

I yelp, then moan against his hand as his fingers curl inside me. His mouth slides up my chest, licking and biting at my overheated flesh before covering my lips.

"Come for me, Princess," he growls, dark and hard and so demanding against my mouth. His fingers pound into me, his thumb sliding over my clit, and my orgasm seizes me in a vice. His mouth absorbs my cries as he frees his cock and slides into me, even with my pussy still trembling and clenching with aftershocks, filling me, stretching me, making me cry out in gratitude and remembered joy.

He pins my hands to the desk with one of his, then presses the other around my throat, cutting off my air just a little, just enough to turn my body to fire and lava and pure, unadulterated pleasure. Fireworks explode behind my eyes, and then I shatter again, coming apart around him, his roar of completion meeting my own cries as our mouths take each other's breath as our own.

We lie there, the glorious weight of him crushing me against the solid bulk of the desk beneath me, gasping for air. I've never felt so sated in my life, as relaxed and sleepy as a day-old kitten.

"I'm going to squash you," he says, and levers himself off me, pulling his clothes back into place.

I sit up and look down at my blouse. All but one button is gone, and that's hanging by a thread. He follows my eyes and smirks. "I'll find you something better to wear."

"Like what?" I sigh. I bought this outfit especially for the gala. As insecure as his comment about buying clothes made me feel, I knew he had a point. If I'd known it was only going to get one outing, I'd have spent less.

He leans over me, one hand braced on either side of my hips, forcing me to lean back. "How about nothing?"

I blink at him and swallow. "What are you saying, Max?"

He leans in, one hand sliding around the nape of my neck, and kisses me, a gentle, exploratory kiss which steals my breath and makes me quiver. "What do you think I'm saying? I've missed you, woman. Don't go. Don't let this be goodbye. Yes, you're the best assistant I've ever had, but you're wasted on me. I know Callie offered you a job."

I gape at him. "How—"

"Princess, she'd be insane not to. Take the job. I always knew you'd be fielding offers like crazy after this event, that's why I said what I did at the hotel. I was an idiot and didn't realise how it would sound and I am so sorry for that. You're too good at what you do to just be my assistant, and you're far too good to be ignored. That's why I knew we wouldn't be working together after this, but please, don't leave me behind."

His other hand strokes over my hip, making me shiver. The way he's touching me, like he can't bear not to, tells me more than words ever could, but it's still so good to hear the words, like a balm healing my aching heart.

"So, you don't want to be my boss anymore?" I smile to show I'm joking, but his face remains serious.

"No, Shay. I just plain want you. And I would be honored if you'd accept these."

He reaches around in his jacket and fishes out a strangely shaped box. It was long and narrow, but quite deep. I frown at him, then open it up.

Inside is my pen, the same one I dropped in the elevator when we first met. I look up at him in shock. "I thought I lost this. How…?"

He looks embarrassed. "I may have taken it off your desk when we headed out to the previous venue, when it had flooded. I knew you were going to end up working for someone else, and I could feel you pulling away from me. I wanted something to remember you by."

I gape at him, then realize there's another, smaller box next to the pen. It's roughly a cube, covered in light blue velvet. My eyes shoot up to his and he reaches out and takes the little box, opening it to reveal a huge diamond ring.

"Shay Thorne, I love you. You're kind and smart and brilliant at your job, not to mention stunningly beautiful. Will you marry me?"

"I...y—"

Suddenly, he pulls me against his chest. "I'm sorry, I'm sorry, we don't have to. We don't have to do anything you don't want."

"Wh—" I push back against him in order to get enough air to speak. "What are you talking about? You don't want to marry me?"

"Of course, I want to marry you, but you're crying, and that's usually a bad thing. I don't want you to cry. I just want to make you happy."

"I am happy, you idiot! And yes, I will marry you. Now put that ring on my finger before I do it myself."

He slides the ring onto my finger, then pulls me close again. "You never have to do it yourself. I'll always be here, for anything you need."

Of all the kisses we've exchanged since meeting, this is the one I'll remember the most, tender yet firm, gentle but strong, with Max's unique taste. I fall into the kiss, knowing it doesn't matter if I lose my balance, because he'll always be there to catch me. Always.

THE END

Read on for a sneak peek of *Leo*, the third book in the Her Dominant Boss series, coming soon on Amazon!

Leo: Her Dominant Boss #3

Charlie

I wince as my '67 Mustang jolts over yet another pothole. This road is for shit, but I'm only an hour or so away from my destination. At least, that's what my cell phone's satellite navigation was telling me up to about twenty minutes ago when the battery died. Now I just have to pray this road spits me out somewhere near a mile marker, or even a sign.

It's after two in the morning, and I know choosing to drive through the night was a bad idea, especially along mountain roads. But dammit, I need this job. An actual paid job as a mechanic is waiting for me in Caulville, as opposed to the eternal unpaid apprenticeship I'm leaving behind.

I'm still pissed about that. I spent the last two years in Craig's auto shop, taking the sexist bullshit that swarms around most any garage, learning everything I could. Pulling all hours, keeping a smile on my face, and maintaining my dad's pride and joy, a cherry red 1967 Mustang fastback, on the side. After a drunk driver strayed onto my parents' side of the road six years ago, this car is all I have left of them. I restored it myself. It's what got me into the classic car restoration business. I was spending so much time around Craig's shop, he said I might as well start learning something.

Not that he's the only person I learned anything from. The internet's a wild and crazy place, all that knowledge just waiting at your fingertips. With my dad's 'stang to practice on, and Craig's employee discount on parts, I've picked up more in the last few years than guys twice my age. Which I know because Wilson, a good ol' boy in his fifties and

Craig's shop manager, is part of the reason I'm now squinting through the windshield at a road which seems determined to destroy my car's suspension before I can reach my destination.

As long as the V-belt holds, we'll make it. I know my car. Which is part of the problem. Wilson doesn't like women who know more than he does about cars. I managed to hide it for the most part, but I think the last straw dropped when a local guy brought his Impala in last week and I had it done in under an hour. A simple fix, but the client left with a smile on his face and my number in his hand. I don't know which part pissed Wilson off more, but I can guess.

Either way, when a job opening came up, I knew it was mine. Right up to the moment Craig told me David got the job. David. A skinny meth-smoking piece of shit who could barely tell the difference between a Shelby and a Barracuda, and never made it to work on time. When I asked him why, he just spouted some bullshit about me being too distracting, and the customers don't want or trust a female mechanic. But I was welcome to stay on as an apprentice, if I wanted.

Whatever. I managed not to quit on the spot. Figured I'd need him for a reference. But as soon as I got home, I pulled out my laptop, another relic from before my parents died, and started looking up jobs. Didn't take long to find this place, well into the next state, where no one's ever heard of Charlotte Hanrahan. I applied under the name of Charlie Hanrahan, though. It's not a lie. I've been called Charlie by pretty much everyone, including my parents, since before I could walk. I wasn't surprised to get accepted within twenty-four hours. Good mechanics are hard to come by and I've worked on exactly the kinds of cars Brent Classics are renowned for doing right by. I mean, it might be a little tough when I get there and the manager finds out I'm a woman, but all I need is a trial run. Once he sees what I can do, he'll have to give me the job.

First I need to get there. By now, I can't be more than twenty minutes away, and I sigh with relief as the cliffs to either side open up and the gradient starts to level out.

And then there's a screeching squeal and my stomach dives straight into my boots.

Oh God. Please no. Don't let it be the V-belt. One of the great things about working at an auto shop is paying cost for any parts you need. But I quit my job there as soon as I got accepted at Brent, which means no more low cost parts, especially the one part I'd known I'd needed but forgot to order in before I left.

Shit. Shit shit shit.

I put the car in park and slide out, pulling my toolbox along with me. I lift the hood and angle the flashlight, praying for all I'm worth. Two seconds later, my stomach rolls over. The belt is clearly visible, frayed and loose. This isn't a clean up job. My V-belt is toast.

The roar of a classic muscle car echoes over the ticking of the hot engine in front of me, and I look up to see headlights approaching. I sigh. I know I should be grateful someone's coming by, but there isn't a chance in hell they'll have the part I need. Maybe I can borrow their phone...to do what? I have no friends, certainly not eight hundred miles from where I used to live, and no money for a tow. I can't leave my classic beauty unattended by the side of the road, even with a messed up V-belt. Someone's sure to 'relocate' it and I'd never see it again. I'm stuck.

I need a new belt, and out here in the middle of nowhere, some time after two in the morning, I haven't the faintest clue how I'm going to get it. I am officially screwed.

***

Leo

I stare at the red lights ahead of me. A classic '67 or '68 Mustang, if I'm not mistaken. Very distinctive taillights. Whoever's driving must be crazy to be out on these roads at this time of night. Not that I can talk, but I know the area. Dad's ruby wedding anniversary gift to my mom, a huge country house, is less than half an hour from here. It made sense when I left the office to stay there instead of at a hotel for the first leg of my trip.

That is, until a massive accident closed the freeway and left me jolting over barely maintained back roads in my Pontiac GTO, the boxes of parts I'm carrying to the shop clanking and sliding around in the trunk. Not that the car can't handle the terrain, but it's not my first choice.

Still, local or not, it doesn't take a rocket scientist to know they could be out here all night. Cell signal is spotty this far out. Chances are, they can't even get a call out for a tow, and it's a pity to see a beautiful car just sitting at the side of the road.

I pull over and check my phone. There's a faint signal, but who knows how long it'll take for a tow truck to get out here? I know I'm just making excuses to go and check out someone else's pretty piece of automotive beauty, but who cares? It's a male bonding thing. I put my hazards on and climb out.

"Hey, need a hand?"

A head appears from under the raised hood of the car, and my first thought is, *that isn't a man*. My second thought isn't really in words, more of a urgent swelling south of my belt buckle, because man, she is *hot*. Huge green eyes lit up like emeralds in the GTO's headlights, full lips, and a body with more curves than the Monaco race track.

And a wrench gripped tight in her left hand.

Shit.

I need to get myself under control. A woman stranded at the side of the road in the middle of the night isn't necessarily going to be happy to see a guy, any guy, let alone one who's clearly very turned on.

I think cold thoughts. Eskimos, igloos, my mom's face when she finds out I've dumped yet another short term fling, and gradually my hard on fades and I figure I can get a little closer to this Mustang-driving goddess without embarrassing myself, or sending her running in a panic.

She hasn't lowered the wrench and I hold my hands up in what I hope is a non-threatening way. At six foot two, it's kind of hard for me, but I'm giving it my best shot. The last thing I want is for her to be scared of me, whether she makes me want to spread her across the hood of her car and eat my fill or not.

"Broke down," she says in a terse voice, clearly not wanting to encourage me. To someone with nine figures in the bank, this is unusual.

"That's a pity," I say. "Anything I can do to help?"

I do my best to keep a light, carefree tone, as I take in the car. The silhouette is stunning. "She's a beauty. Sixty-seven?"

I look back at her in time to see her eyebrows twitch and even from here I can see her pupils dilate. She's got a good look at me and now she's not quite as uninterested.

"Yeah. My dad's." She's still working on that back off tone, even though I can see a spark in her eyes. Then she looks back at the engine beside her and her lips twist with regret. "V-belt blew. I've been meaning to order it in but unless you've got one of those in the back seat..." She sighs.

This is an unusual situation for me. The woman is genuinely more interested in her car than she is in me, and she's pretty damn interested in me.

"Well, I don't have one in my back seat," I tell her, and I'm rewarded with a smile that short-circuits my brain. I stare at her as fireworks go off behind my eyes, then shake my head and pull myself together. "But I do have one in the trunk."

Her look of absolute shock is worth it and I'm sorry I have to turn away in order to get the part from the trunk. I saunter up to her, holding it out and she stares at it, then looks up at me, her lips parting on a gasp as she takes me in.

"I'm not even going to ask why you have one of these. Just... th-thank you," she stammers, dragging her eyes from the belt, and my chest, up to my eyes. "I can't pay for it, though. I-I'm...between jobs at the minute."

"That's okay. Consider it a gift. I've got three more of them back there."

I grin down at her and she smiles, then reaches for the part but I shake my head.

"The least I can do for a lady is fit it," I tell her, and something flickers behind her eyes. If I didn't know better, I'd say it was disappointment, which doesn't make sense because any women I know would jump at the chance for a guy to get covered in engine grease instead of them.

This girl just keeps on surprising me.

Coming soon on Amazon!

ABOUT THE AUTHOR

K.R. Max loves ice cream, big fluffy dogs, and stories where the woman finds her place with a super-hot guy who adores her. She specializes in dominant heroes and the sweet, innocent women who bring them to their knees!

If you like a fast read with a guaranteed happy ever after, lots of super-hot and VERY dirty shenanigans, and NO cheating OR cliffhangers, K. R. Max is for you!

You can find her on Facebook, at
http://www.facebook.com/krmaxwrites/

You can also sign up for her mailing list at
http://eepurl.com/cOtnGz

CPSIA information can be obtained
at www.ICGtesting.com
Printed in the USA
LVHW110150270121
677620LV00011B/190

9 781694 509567